W9-CED-246

Perfect Puppy

To Charlie's Family,
Try not to eat
your homework!
Thomas F. Yezerski

by Stephanie Calmenson

Illustrated by Thomas F. Yezerski

Clarion Books • New York

To Zoë May

—S. C.

To Tiffy and Mickey

—T. F. Y.

Clarion Books
a Houghton Mifflin Company imprint
215 Park Avenue South, New York, NY 10003

The illustrations were executed in watercolor.
The text was set in 16-point Triplex serif.

www.houghtonmifflinbooks.com

Printed in Singapore.

Library of Congress Cataloging-in-Publication Data

Calmenson, Stephanie.
Perfect puppy / by Stephanie Calmenson ; illustrated by Thomas F. Yezerski.
p. cm.
Summary: A little puppy wants to be perfect so that his owner will always love him, and even though he makes mistakes, he learns that he is loved anyway.
ISBN 0-618-01139-0
[1. Dogs—Fiction. 2. Animals—Infancy—Fiction.] I. Yezerski, Thomas, ill. II. Title.

PZ7.C136 Pe 2001 [E]—dc21 00-065732

TWP 10 9 8 7 6 5 4 3 2 1

DOG

I am going to be the perfect puppy.
I will never make any mistakes.

If I am perfect, my girl will take good care of me.
She will feed me.

Yum!
Yum!
Yum!

She will walk me.

This way!
That way!
This way!
That way!

She will rub my belly.

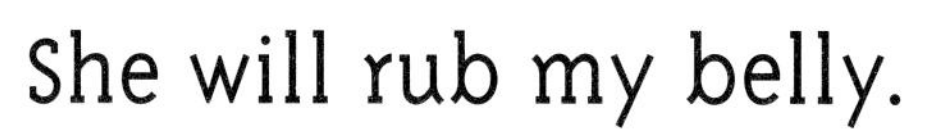

Ooh, that feels nice!
HAPPY BIRTHDAY

She will love me so much!

I'm a lucky puppy!
Here I come!

I am going to start being perfect right away.
First, I will be housebroken.

MY PUPPY
NG CALL

You missed the paper, Puppy!
Puddles? What puddles?

I will be a very good listener.

Puppy, sit!
I learn fast, right?

I will be a super helper.

Fetch the shoe!
Fetch and chew?
I can do that!

I will help without even being asked.
I will be the perfect puppy vacuum cleaner.

Goodbye, cookie crumbs!
COOKIES

I will be the perfect puppy paper shredder.

Goodbye, big papers!

I will do amazing tricks.
I will win exciting prizes.

I have to sneeze.

I will be the most perfect puppy who ever lived!

FIRST PRIZE
Thank you!
Thank you!
BEST IN SHOW

PUPPY, NO!
YOU ATE MY HOMEWORK!

Help, I made a mistake!

Being perfect is too hard.

I'm leaving.

What will happen to me now?
Who will take care of me?

Who will love me?
I don’t know!

I'm scared.

I give up.
My paws are muddy.
I have a flea.
I'll just lie here forever and drool.

I'm so lonely!

Wait . . . What's this?
I hear someone calling.
It's my girl.

Puppy, where are you?
Come back!

Here she is!
I'm getting my belly rubbed!
How can this be happening
when I'm a muddy, drooly, fleabitten mess?

I can't believe it.

My girl is talking to me.
Her voice is gentle.

Thank goodness
I found you!

We're going home.

This way! This way!

I'm getting a bubble bath.

So long, flea!

Here comes my after-bath treat.

Yum!

My girl wants me to keep her company.

I have to write my homework over.
I will not eat that. I will not eat that.
MATH

She's talking to me.
I can tell she's saying nice things.

You're so sweet and cuddly.
You're furry and funny.
You've got big brown eyes,
a cold wet nose,
a pink tongue,
a waggy tail.
I'm all ears!

I love you so much!

I am her perfect puppy.